The Mysterious Lake
OTRIANA

BY:

HELEN KELTIE

Copyright © 2022 Helen Keltie

All rights reserved. No part of this book may be used or reproduced by any means, graphic, electronic, or mechanical, including photocopying, recording, taping or by any information storage retrieval system without the written permission of the author except in the case of brief quotations embodied in critical articles and reviews.

Proisle Publishing Service
1177 Avenue of the Americas, 5th Floor, New York, NY 10036, USA
info@proislepublishing.com

Because of the dynamic nature of the Internet, any web addresses or links contained in this book may have changed since publication and may no longer be valid. The views expressed in this work are solely those of the author and do not necessarily reflect the views of the publisher, and the publisher hereby disclaims any responsibility for them.

ISBN: 978-1-959449-27-0

PROISLE PUBLISHING

Table of Contents

Chapter 1: 6
Chapter 2: 11
Chapter 3: 13
Chapter 4: 17
Chapter 5: 22
Chapter 6: 24
Chapter 7: 27
Chapter 8: 30
Chapter 9: 36
Chapter 10: 39
Chapter 11: 41
Chapter 12: 44
Chapter 13: 49
Chapter 14: 53
Chapter 15: 57
Chapter 16: 60
Chapter 17: 64
Chapter 18: 67
Chapter 19: 69

To Leanne for encouraging me
to get the book published

Thank you to Carolyn for co-editing
and typing up the manuscript

Chapter 1

Miffy, Ted Brown's little terrier, had disappeared and now he was scouring the bush looking for her. Katie and Josh told him they had heard a dog barking in the bush two days ago.

Katie and Josh are the ten-year old Jenkins twins with brown hair and masses of freckles. Josh had hazel eyes and Katie's were the colour of emeralds.

"Don't tell Mum and Dad, Mr. Brown. We're not supposed to go there."

"Don't worry Katie, I won't say a word."

Just recently, the bush had been the scene of small animals disappearing. Looking around him, he noticed a large pool of water ahead of him.

"I don't remember seeing that before." He was puzzled. There were no reflections of tree branches or the scudding clouds overhead. As he leaned over, he whistled. There was no reflection of him!

Katie and Josh decided to have another look for Miffy after school. "We'd better not be too long or Mum will want to know where we've been," Katie said

Josh nodded his head, "We'll just walk through the bush".

When they reached the water, Josh became excited, "Look Katie, the muddy edge has paw prints." Josh found a small pebble which he dropped into the lake. Immediately the lake opened. Watery fingers fluttered along the edge of the lake, smoothing away the paw prints.

The children could hear a dog barking. Drawing closer to the lake, Josh said, "That's Miffy!" He looked at Katie, "She's down there". His feet slipped in the mud and he fell into the water. Katie grabbed his arm and was pulled in with him. They fell a long way before they reached the bottom. The world around them was a swirling mass of pearly grey and misty blue light.

Katie felt her neck. She had grown gills like a fish. As she looked at Josh, she saw that he also had gills and his skin was covered with silver scales. Silvery scales were growing rapidly all over her body.

"Don't be frightened children. You'll need these minor adjustments when you visit Otriana. That is the name of this world."

A tall woman with fine floating seaweed for hair and silvery blue scales covering her body was smiling at them. She wore a loose white cloak, which floated around her, "If you're looking for your little dog, here she is." Miffy seemed pleased to see them. She no longer had fur, but was covered in fine brown seaweed and sported tiny black gills. Josh picked up Miffy and cuddled her.

Katie was frightened. "We must go home. Tell us how to get back please."

The woman laughed softly, "All in good time. Come home with me. You can play with my children for a little while." She rang a crystal bell that hung around her neck. Two huge seahorses floated into view pulling a large shell. The shell had seating for four people. The woman beckoned, "My name is Meerlyn. I live a short distance away. The seahorses will take us there."

The seahorses swam swiftly and after a few minutes, stopped before a turreted house, which was built of white coral. The front door was a huge pearl. Meerlyn opened the door. The children hesitated.

Josh whispered, "Don't eat or drink anything."

"I won't," replied Katie.

They entered the house. Meerlyn was cuddling a little girl who looked exactly like her mother. Standing on her right was a boy about twelve years old. His skin consisted of brown scales and his eyes were a vivid blue.

"My son Nepta and little Coralie." She placed Coralie on the floor and set a table with fine goblets and a plate of biscuits. "Come, eat and drink. You must be thirsty and tired." Meerlyn picked up Coralie and glided from the room.

Nepta hissed, "You cannot stay here. Do NOT drink or eat anything. You must leave this house before my father comes home or you will never leave... and take the dog with you!"

Nepta led them to the front door. It was locked. "I have the key." He unlocked the door and pointed to the road, "Follow this road to the left until you come to a jetty. The boatmen will row you across to the headland. Climb the hill. Ahead you will see a volcano. It spurts jets of water every half hour. You must climb the volcano. The water jets will carry you back to your world." He turned away. "I wish you luck. I don't want to see you here again. You are in danger."

When the children reached the jetty, the boatmen were waiting for them. Very quickly, they arrived at the headland. Once they climbed the hill, they saw the volcano ahead. Glancing behind, they could see lights flashing. The children realized that people were searching for them. Climbing up the mountain was painfully hard. Miffy was running ahead. The searchers were closing in. Katie didn't think they would reach the summit in time.

"We're there, Katie," Josh gasped. "I don't know how long we have to wait before the next jet of water." He was trembling and continually looking behind him. Josh caught hold of Miffy.

The howling mob was halfway up the mountainside. Some of the figures appeared like snakes. They were gaining rapidly. The volcano shook and rumbled, then 'whoosh'! A jet of water spurted upward. Without hesitation, Josh threw himself into the water and screamed to Katie, "Hurry up or they'll catch you!"

Katie shut her eyes. Wailing and shouting reached her ears. Fingers clutched her left foot. She felt the scales being ripped off. As she was borne upwards, the pain in her left foot almost caused her to faint. She was thrown on top of Josh, knocking the breath from his body. Miffy was shivering. They lay still for a few minutes. Katie's left foot was bleeding and there were deep gouges. Josh was unharmed and relieved to be back in his own world.

"I can't walk!" Katie was sobbing.

Josh looked around, "We're back where the lake was. It's shrinking!"

"Go home, Josh. Get Dad. I'll be alright with Miffy."

Josh didn't have far to walk. His father and Mr. Brown were looking for them. They could hear Miffy barking.

Eight hundred kilometers away, people were remarking about the sudden appearance of a huge lake. A boy with vivid blue eyes was often seen wandering along its shores.

Chapter 2

Katie's mother was worried. Katie would wake night after night screaming and sobbing. "My darling, hush." Sally Jenkins held Katie close to her and rocked backwards and forwards on the bed until Katie calmed down.

The injury to her foot had taken weeks to heal. The doctor was puzzled. "I've never seen wounds like it," he repeatedly told Katie's parents. Josh was quiet. He was very worried about his sister. He had explained their adventure to his parents and Mr. Brown. Only Mr. Brown seemed to understand.

"Miffy is quieter, she doesn't bark so much." He shook his head. "She absolutely hates water." He had taken her to the vet.

"Ted, she's undernourished. I can't find anything else wrong with her. Feed her up and, if you are still worried, bring her back to me." The vet was puzzled.

Ted had questioned the children and seemed to understand. "I believe your story, mainly because of Miffy's behaviour and Katie's wounds. I have been on the internet and a market town called Briesdale has reported a mysterious lake that has just suddenly appeared. It's on the other side of the state. I'm going to have a look at it." He hesitated, "People have seen a strange boy with vivid blue eyes wandering around the lake's perimeter".

"That's Nepta," Josh interrupted. "He helped us. Perhaps he might come back with you."

Ted Brown considered. If Nepta did come back with him, it could be a healing process, or it could make matters worse? He patted Josh on the head. "I'll see. I can't make him come. Of course, if he's been exiled from his world... well, we'll have to wait and see."

Ted Brown looked at Katie. Her eyes betrayed her. Poor kid, she was really scared. He wondered if he should take Miffy. On consideration, she would be unhappy if he left her with friends. As long as he didn't take her to the lake, it would be OK.

The next week was school holidays. Josh asked his parents if he could go with Mr. Brown. Ted thought it might be a good idea. Nepta would recognize Josh and maybe there would be a happy outcome. Josh's father, Jack Jenkins, was doubtful, but as Josh didn't seem to be any the worse after the adventure, he reluctantly agreed. As he was owed some time off from the office, he decided he would accompany them.

"You'll be able to watch Miffy. She trusts you Josh." Mr. Brown smiled. Josh nodded his head. He was excited and hoped to meet up with Nepta again.

Chapter 3

Briesdale was a bustling town and by mid-afternoon, Mr. Brown had driven to a motel in the Centre of the town. "We'll make some enquiries first, Jack. Tomorrow, we'll drive out to the lake and see what develops." Jack nodded his head in agreement.

Josh was a mixture of nervousness and excitement. "Whatever you say, Mr. Brown." He was cuddling Miffy. She appeared to be totally relaxed, "Is she eating OK?"

"Not really Josh. I can't find any food she seems to like. Of course, we don't know what she experienced in Otriana." He stroked Miffy and sighed. "The motel proprietor said, "Yes, I've seen the lake. I didn't see any boy wandering around. Funny thing though, the water is clear, but there are no reflections."

Ted Brown muttered, "That's one thing I do know, no reflections. It has got to be the same."

Josh was frowning. "Perhaps we won't meet up with Nepta," he paused. "Could be someone else?" His hazel eyes were troubled.

Mr. Brown put his arm around Josh's shoulders, "Let's go and find out. We may have to go every day and wait for hours. Come along son."

When they reached the lake, everything was quiet. The three of them walked a little way around the lake. A bird swooped down to drink. The waters parted and the bird disappeared. Josh gasped.

Mr. Brown muttered softly, "I see what you mean. Let's go as close as we can and look in. If Nepta's there, he may see you."

Josh started to tremble. The horrifying memories came back. His legs refused to move. "I can't, Mr. Brown. I'm scared."

"Alright Josh, stay here with your Dad, I'll go." He squeezed Josh's shoulders and slowly walked to the edge of the lake. He waited a little while then called softly, "Nepta, if you can hear me, I've got Josh here. He'd like to talk to you."

The water rippled and a voice came through the lake. "I'm Nepta. I can't come now. Wait for a while. Let me see Josh. Is he alright?"

Ted beckoned to Josh, "Nepta's here. He wishes to see you."

Josh crept to the lake's edge and looked in. His eyes met Nepta's. "Nepta, are you in trouble?"

Nepta appeared to have been crying, "Josh, I've sneaked out from my home. My father is very angry with me. My mother has made me promise not to let any travellers go in future." He looked down. "Sometimes the water will let me through. Otriana has a mind of her own. Wait Josh, I think the path is clear."

Nepta's head and shoulders broke the surface. "Don't touch me. I'll get out." Slowly he rose and eventually was able to stand on dry land. The brown scales on his body and the fish gills disappeared. His head lost the seaweed and coarse reddish brown hair appeared. He laughed, "I'm almost one of you."

Ted and Jack were dumbfounded!

"This is my father," Josh introduced them.

"How's your dog?" Nepta was looking at Miffy.

"Miffy belongs to Mr. Brown. We think she's dying."

Nepta put his hand in his pocket. He pulled out a water-logged biscuit. "Here Miffy, eat this." Miffy came forward and sniffed the biscuit. She gingerly bit and swallowed. Nepta patted her, "She'll be alright now. My father would only feed her our food. He didn't want Miffy at our place, but my sister Coralie loved her."

They continued to walk along the lake's shore. Nepta queried, "You have a sister Josh. Is she well?"

Josh replied, "No she isn't. She has terrible nightmares and the scales were ripped from her foot. Her foot is only just starting to heal."

Nepta stopped suddenly. Turning to Josh, he said. "You will need to come back with me to Otriana. I can give you something that will help her."

He looked enquiringly at Josh's father. Jack Jenkins wasn't too happy about this turn of events, but he stated that he and Josh would accompany Nepta. He would do anything to help his daughter.

"How long will this take?"

"About an hour in your time. I will have to alter your appearance. Do you trust me?"

Josh's father sighed, "So be it."

Nepta looked at them all. "Take my hand." He walked them all into the water. As the water closed over them, Nepta muttered words in a strange language. Ted, Jack and Josh found they were turning into fish. Josh became a silver fish, Ted and Jack were silver fish with gold fins and Miffy turned into a sea slug. Nepta laughed, "Don't be scared. You will return to normal when you return to the surface. I had to change your appearance. My people would never let you go again. I can only work limited transformations."

Josh, his father and Ted wanted to ask questions, but found they couldn't talk. Miffy was quiet, so obviously she couldn't bark. When they reached the floor of the lake, a large sea dragon was waiting for them.

"Nepta, if that's all you can bring back, I won't let you surface again," it roared. "Father, there's nothing much up there."

"Well, we'll cook the fish for dinner. They look plump enough and will make a reasonable meal. I'm surprised the sea slug was up at the surface. Is it a plaything? It can find its own way about. Come Nepta. Ride on my back. Your mother wants you home."

Chapter 4

Nepta's father produced a net and scooped up the fish. Ted, Jack and Josh waited for an opportunity to escape the net. Ted looked back to where Miffy was lying on the sand. There was nothing he could do. He watched the little sea slug burrow into the sand. Josh's father was suspicious. This was probably a trick and they would all be killed. He should never have agreed to this mad scheme. If Nepta was to be trusted, he was their only means of escape. Josh wanted to yell and his silvery body wriggled and squirmed, but the net held them tight. Josh saw the coral house loom out of the mist ahead. Meerlyn was waiting at the front door with Coralie.

"We'll have fish for dinner my dear, all that Nepta could find." Nepta's father was changing shape. The sea dragon's appearance changed to a tall man with brown green scales, thick brown seaweed for hair and a bushy beard. He picked up Coralie and entered the house. Throwing the net on the table, he turned to Meerlyn, "I need to go out again. I shall be back in a little while." He sat Coralie on a low stool and left the house.

"Mother, may we substitute the fish? These are earth people. I had to change them." He explained the situation to Meerlyn.

She was horrified, "If your father finds out, he will never let you leave the house." She wrung her hands, "What can I do?"

Nepta thought hard. "I can speak to Wizen. He'll conjure up look-a-like fish and he can return these people to normal. I want some medicine for the girl who was here."

Meerlyn moaned, "Oh Nepta! I'm going to lose you. You'll never be able to stay here." She burst out crying and rushed from the room.

Nepta carefully picked up the net and quietly left the house. Muttering more strange words, he turned himself into a giant groper. Opening his mouth, he took in the net and carried the burden in his jaws. Josh, Ted and Jack were terrified. Expecting to be cooked and eaten, they now faced being swallowed by the groper. It was pitch black inside, only the luminescence of their scales showed any light.

After some time, the groper opened its jaws and spat out the net. Nepta changed back to his boyish form again and faced a merman with a flowing white beard and long white hair.

"Wizen, I need your help."

Wizen opened his green eyes wide, "Nepta, you're back with us. I've missed you my boy. What can I do for you?" Nepta explained the situation. "Ho-ho, how I'd love to see your father's face. Poor old Bragh." Wizen quietened down. "But what about you lad? If this is discovered, your fate is sealed."

Nepta shrugged his shoulders, "Perhaps I could live with the earth people." Tears sparkled in his eyes.

Wizen rumpled the seaweed on his head. "Let's think about this."

He drew three fish shapes in the sand. Waving his left hand over them, three live fish appeared and they were replicas of the earthling fish in every detail. He opened the net and Josh, Ted and Jack floated out. The other three fish were caught and placed in the net.

"Nepta, your friends can stay here for the moment. I can't change them back just yet. It's too dangerous. Take these fish home. They won't taste good." He chuckled, "That will teach Bragh a lesson." He shook with laughter as Nepta turned towards home. "Now, my fine three. I'll give you back your voices. I look forward to an evening's entertainment."

Wizen lived alone in a well-lit cave. There were beautiful coral columns throughout the cave. As water flowed around them, it sounded like a harp. Comfortable chairs were placed around the cave and there was a passing parade of brightly coloured fish. Wizen nodded to the three, "Make yourselves as comfortable as you can. You are probably wondering why I am helping Nepta. His father and I grew up together and he was always a bully and a show-off. How he managed to snare Meerlyn I'll never know." He pulled a huge pot off a glowing fire and rumbled, "Not like your fire on earth, but it gives out heat and is good for cooking. We call it Glofa. You can safely eat this. It won't harm you." He ladled out four serves into large shells.

"There are no spoons, you can drink it." He placed the shells on a bench and invited them to drink.

Josh's father thought Wizen sounded trustworthy, so he lapped up several mouthfuls of soup. His hunger was satisfied and nothing alarming happened. He nodded to the others, then tried his voice, "Come on Josh and Ted, it's safe and tastes good."

Wizen arranged himself in an armchair, "I don't carry on the wild practices like the other folks here. Travellers are always welcome and if they can return safely, all well and good. Now, when you've finished and feel up to it, I'd like to hear your stories."

Josh's father nudged him, "You tell it son. After all, it's your adventure."

Josh explained what happened when he and Katie were last here. When he finished, Wizen was frowning, "Bragh would never forgive Nepta, that's why he was punished. Bragh was after the children. He likes to capture the children from earth, but luckily, very few come here."

Ted Brown asked, "What happens to the children?"

Wizen looked at him beneath lowered eyes for a moment. "He makes slaves out of them. They work very hard and when they displease him, he turns them into sea snakes and they live out a miserable existence."

Josh, Ted and Jack shuddered. Ted asked, "What about the small animals and birds?"

"Oh, they're eaten. Your Miffy was lucky that Coralie took a fancy to her." Ted wondered if he could find Miffy again. He put the question to Wizen. "Sea slugs don't move very fast and she's probably still in the same area. We'll go and look for her tomorrow. It is dark now and there are dangers I don't want to face. Rest if you can." Wizen swam through an opening and the light dimmed.

Chapter 5

The following morning, the trio followed in Wizen's wake and searched the sandy bottom for Miffy. There were plenty of sea slugs, but as Wizen touched them, they just curled into themselves. Wizen was becoming worried, "Nepta's father may return here soon. I suggest you hide in the heavier seaweed. I'll continue looking."

The three swam into the forest of seaweed just in time. Nepta's father appeared, "Looking for something in particular Wizen?"

Wizen faced him squarely. "Yes and it's none of your business."

Nepta's father hissed, "I think I can guess… fish and a sea slug? Nepta has been to see you. No wonder the fish tasted like sand." He came up close to Wizen. "I'll find them, I'll have you watched old friend. They won't escape a second time." Suddenly he yelled, "Something bit me." He stamped his foot down hard. Wizen noticed a slight movement in the sand near Bragh's left foot. He remained silent but watchful. Bragh strode away, "Be warned Wizen. These travellers belong to me."

After Bragh had gone, Wizen raked the sand with his fingers. He secured a small brown sea slug and he called softly, "Ted, call your dog's name."

Ted whispered, "Miffy?" The sea slug wiggled and turned towards Ted. Wizen muttered a few words and there stood Miffy, a seaweed covered terrier again. Wizen placed her in his cloak. Coming close to the forest of seaweed, he said quietly, "You three had better stay here. Bragh will be watching my cave. I'll return as soon as I can." Wizen drifted away, taking Miffy with him.

The trio were still in trouble, "How are we ever going to get out of this?" Jack Jenkins was very angry. "If I could only get my normal shape back I could do something."

Ted Brown was thinking, "We have to stay here until he returns. I hope that by tonight we may be free. Shhh, I hear something." A large groper floated nearby. His sense of smell detected the fish, but he couldn't break through the seaweed. He hovered there watching the seaweed.

"Nepta, is that you?" Josh called softly. The groper swam closer and peered into the dark shapes of seaweed. "Shhh Josh! Do you want to get us killed?' asked his father.

Ted Brown was watching the groper, "Shhh, it's not Nepta! We mustn't talk anymore."

They swam deeper into the forest. Suddenly the bright light of an electric eel danced around them. She swam up close and stopped. "My, it's Wizen's visitors. I noticed you last night when I swam past his cave." She laughed shrilly, "Where's the old fool gone? You'll be eaten alive out here. In fact I might even shock you and taste you myself." She raised her head to strike!

Chapter 6

Sally Jenkins had expected to hear from her husband. He had phoned when they arrived in Briesdale. Forty-eight hours had passed and she had heard nothing since. When she phoned the motel, all the manager could tell her was that the menfolk had all driven out to the lake and had not returned. Katie was almost hysterical. "Look darling, Mr. Brown and your father know what they're doing and Josh is very capable. I'm sure they will be alright." She sat Katie on her knee and cuddled her. She didn't tell Katie that she was very worried.

Wizen arrived back at the cave. He noticed that there were a larger number of fish swimming past. "Mmmm Bragh, you have your spies out already." He entered the cave and pulled a screen over the entrance. He went into the inner room, which was quite dark. This room was Wizen's sleeping quarters. The only furniture was a huge bed. He laid his cloak on the bed and unwrapped Miffy. Her soft brown eyes almost made his heart break. "Sorry, little one, I'll have to change you again." He waved his left hand over Miffy and she transformed into green seaweed. He placed her amongst his other pots of seaweed and gently stroked the leaves.

"Your roots will find nourishment and you'll be safe here." He left the cave and gave a piercing whistle. A giant manta ray emerged from the gloom. Wizen climbed on its back and was borne swiftly to the mountains. Telling the manta ray to wait, he hurried to a clump of coral and called softly, "Mary-Anna, if you're home, come here. I have urgent business."

"It must be urgent if you have to fly here Uncle." The loveliest mermaid glided out from behind the coral. She had long fair hair and sea-green eyes, which sparkled with laughter. "You should come here and live with us, Uncle. Leave that gloomy old cave."

"We've been through all this before. I'm content where I am. Now listen, this is the reason for my visit."

Mary-Anna was thoughtful, "The only way we will return these people will be in the night." She shuddered, "Even Bragh doesn't emerge then." She ran her fingers through her hair. "It will be dangerous. The sea monsters prowl at night."

Wizen sighed, "I know that, but if we reach the other side of the mountains, we'll join the whales in the deeper water and they can transport the earthlings back to the surface."

Mary-Anna wrinkled her white brow, "Can you summon Umiel? She is quick, cunning and will try anything."

Wizen replied, "I'll try, but that sprite stays just under the surface. She should be an air sprite like her sister, Ariel."

"You must return Uncle. Bragh will be sending his spies here." She linked her arm in his, "Tell Nepta to join us here. We'll make him welcome and he can stay here as long as he likes. Bragh generally doesn't worry us."

Wizen nodded, "Poor lad, he'll need a home. He has Meerlyn's kinder nature." He waved farewell, but before he climbed on the manta ray's back, he noticed a moray eel lurking around the coral. He wondered how much it had heard and took a closer look. The eel was thin and had sad eyes. He muttered a few words and the eel changed into a young woman. He jumped back, "An earthling!"

"Oh sir, please help me," She fell on her knees.

Mary-Anna took her hand and helped her to her feet, "Come, eat and rest. I will take care of you."

Chapter 7

The electric eel hovered. Jack, Ted and Josh were paralyzed with fear as they watched the eel rear back. As she brought her head down, a thick band of seaweed wrapped itself around her head and was instantly incinerated. The trio swam for their lives. They penetrated the darker forest of seaweed and eventually came out into the light. Gasping and shaking uncontrollably, they stopped and looked behind them. No eel followed.

An almost transparent fairy-like creature was curled up in the highest seaweed tips. "I'm Umiel. Come up here and let me look at you. Who's been chasing you I wonder?" She laughed merrily. Her laughter sounded like tinkling wind chimes. When they had recovered their breath, they floated up to her.

The sunlight was sparkling through the water. Josh said, "We need to find Wizen."

Umiel laughed again, "Fish who can talk! I can see Wizen's hand in this." She gave the three a piercing look, "Ah, but you're not fish." The three felt their hearts sink. Another trap? Surely not with someone who could laugh like that? She seemed to be able to read their minds, "Don't worry, I won't give you away. Follow me and I'll take you to Wizen. He's returning from the mountains. I don't think you should go back to the cave as its being watched."

She flew off to the right and they followed. They crossed dwellings and coral reefs. Eventually they saw the mountain range ahead. A dark speck was moving rapidly towards them. As it drew closer, they recognized Wizen riding a giant manta ray. When he reached them, he told the ray to stop, "Umiel, I was looking for you. I need your help."

Umiel asked, "And what is my payment?"

Wizen looked at her under his bushy eyebrows, "Name something you really desire."

Umiel answered, "You have a little dog, a terrier. I've watched them from the surface. I want one as a companion."

Ted cried out, "No, not my Miffy!"

Umiel's voice became icy, "If you want my help to return to your world, you must pay me. I want your dog."

Josh whispered to Ted, "We can't return home Mr. Brown, unless we give her what she wants. I imagine she could be very dangerous."

Ted didn't answer. He was thinking... I knew I shouldn't have brought her. He looked at Josh, "If Miffy wasn't here, she might have asked for you." Josh shuddered.

Ted said to Umiel, "Promise me that you will take care of her. If you tire of her, return her to me."

Umiel nodded solemnly, "Agreed. When you hear wind chimes round your door, look for your dog." She snickered, "But I want her for keeps."

Wizen thought it was time to speak up. "You will not receive Miffy until all these people are safely returned to their world."

"So be it!" She snapped.

Chapter 8

Ariel had seen the earthlings enter the water with Nepta. She wondered how they were. Ariel was a tiny, fairy-like creature and when the sun shone on her, her wings sparkled of blue, red and gold. She understood the boy and his father were worried about a woman and a little girl. "I'll speak to my friend, the West Wind. He will suggest they come here. I hope I am doing the right thing."

Sally Jenkins had been listening to the wind rustling the leaves as branches tapped on the window. She made up her mind. "Katie, we'll go to Briesdale. I can't stand this waiting about. We may be more useful there and able to help in some way. I'll pack our things and we'll take Dad's car."

Katie nodded her head. Her eyes filled with tears. She was missing her Dad and Josh badly. "Mum, we won't go near the lake, will we?" She was hesitant and very frightened.

"Darling, you can stay in the car at all times, but I will have to drive out to the lake."

The motel manager had been in contact with the police and Ted Brown's truck had been towed back to a garage. The police could not find any clues to the mysterious disappearance of the two men and a boy. Sally looked at Katie, "This is just not like your father."

Katie thought they had all entered the lake and now they couldn't get back. "O-h-h Dad and Josh, be careful!"

When Sally and Katie arrived in Briesdale, the motel manager was relieved to see them. "I'm sorry I can't give you any further news. I've even driven out there, but there's absolutely nothing to see." Ariel was watching for them when they came out of the motel. She sat on the car roof until they reached the lake.

"Kat-ee, Kat-ee", she called softly. "Your brother, father and friend are still safe."

Katie climbed out of the car. "Mum, come with me to the water. I'm not touching it, but I want to have a look."

Sally Jenkins paused, "Are you sure? You know how terrified you've been."

Katie smiled, "I'm sure."

Ariel flew over the water. "Umiel, if you hear me, Josh's sister and his mother are here. Speak to me."

Katie peered fearfully into the water. There was nothing. Her mother held her hand. "We'll drive back to the motel and rest. A meal and a good sleep will refresh us."

They returned to the lake the following morning. Sally had packed a picnic lunch. "We'll drive around the lake, Katie. We may see more on the far side."

The sun was shining on the water and Katie noticed some ripples when they had driven halfway. "Mum, stop the car!"

Sally braked but kept the motor running. "What did you see?" She looked anxiously at the water. A man was swimming towards them. In two or three strokes, he would be at the water's edge. Katie held her breath. Sally exclaimed, "It's Ted!" She looked for her husband and Josh. Ted Brown was alone. Ted's clothes were torn in many places. He fell on the ground and lay still. "Stay here, Katie. I'll see if he's alright." Sally ran across to Ted and shook his shoulders. "Ted, can you speak? Are you all right? Where are the others?"

Ted groaned. He sat up with difficulty, "Oh Sally, it's you." He put his head in his hands.

"Ted, tell me. Where are Jack and Josh?"

Ted muttered, "Give me a minute, Sally. I'm exhausted." He flopped back on the ground. Sally returned to the car and fetched a travelling rug.

Katie was tense, "Mum, what's happened?

"I don't know yet. Ted is exhausted. He'll talk to us when he can. Stay there darling." Ted was shivering. Sally folded the rug around him. "I'll bring you a cup of coffee. That will help to warm you up."

She returned with the coffee and he sipped it slowly, "Ahh, that's better". He glanced at Sally and frowned, "Drive me back to town, Sally. I'll shower and then I'll tell you what's happening. Alas, Jack and Josh are still in the lake, but friends are working to help them escape." He finished the coffee and staggered back to the car. He nodded to Katie and collapsed on the seat.

After Ted had eaten and rested, he continued the story. "There's a fairy-like creature named Umiel in the water. I don't know if she can be trusted. She promised to help us all escape on one condition," his voice broke and he looked away. "She's keeping Miffy".

"Oh Mr. Brown, is there no way you can get her back?" Katie was horrified.

"Shhh Katie, let Mr. Brown finish." Sally put her arm around Katie's shoulders.

Ted continued, "She took me to some lava tubes. They are crumbling, but we found one that I could swim up. She wanted me out of the way so she could take Miffy. I wanted to send Josh up first, but she wouldn't hear of it." He paused. He could understand how Sally and Katie must be feeling and he felt guilty for leaving the others behind.

He hesitated, "Unfortunately, the lava tube collapsed behind me, so no one else can come up that way again. There may be other tubes. I hope so for Josh and Jack's sake. Another friend is a merman called Wizen. I trust him completely. I know you won't stop worrying, but with Wizen, there is hope. I doubt if the police would believe such a story as this and I could be in serious trouble."

Sally said, "I noticed your skin through the torn clothing. You have infected wounds which need attention. See a doctor. He may be able to help and confirm your story with the police."

"I'll go tomorrow." He stood up and walked a few paces, "Sally, I know you must feel I've deserted your husband and Josh, but they both urged me to go. One less for Wizen to worry about and I may be able to help up here."

Sally's face was grim as she said to Katie, "We'll drive out to the lake again. I don't suppose there's anything we can do. It's been three days now since they disappeared." They had just reached the car when Katie noticed a flash of blue and gold. Ariel caught her attention. "My sister Umiel lives in the lake. That man mentioned her."

Sally and Katie could see a tiny figure with gauzy wings sitting on the leaves of a low hanging branch. Together they cried, "We see you."

"Look for me out at the lake. I'll leave a sign for you. I'll help you where I can, but Otriana is not my world. I prefer the air and the sunlight." She flew off.

Sally shook her head, "This becomes more unbelievable every minute."

Katie was smiling, "It'll be alright Mum. I feel we can trust her."

When they arrived at the lake, it was in turmoil. The water was boiling. A roaring noise could be heard in the Centre of the lake. Katie and her mother watched in horror as a huge sea dragon's head emerged. Arial flew to the windscreen, "Drive back. Go! Go quickly!" She flew back towards the town.

The sea dragon was coming towards them. Quickly, Sally reversed the car and swung away. Alas, the wheels caught in a rut and the car stalled. A black shadow overhung the car and the door on Katie's side was ripped off. "Mum, help me!" she screamed. Sally caught hold of Katie, but the sea dragon swiped her away and clawed Sally's arm. In a flash, Katie was gone with the monster. Sally looked at the lake. Ripples were spreading out from the Centre. Her arm was aching and blood was oozing from her claw marks. She fainted.

Chapter 9

Wizen was aghast when Umiel had told him Katie had been captured by Bragh. She spoke with a certain amount of malice, "Now what do you do, old man?" She waited patiently. Wizen was thinking… the nearest lava tubes are by the mountains. If I can transport the boy and his father to them, then I need only worry about the girl.

"What about my payment for helping you?" Umiel snapped.

Wizen spoke sternly, "Only when these three are returned to their world and not before. That was the agreement."

Umiel tried to read his mind and failed. He had installed a magic locking device on the screen over his cave entrance. Only he could unlock it. He whistled again and the giant manta ray swam towards him. He asked if the earthlings were safe.

"Yes Wizen. The earthlings are where you left them. No one has noticed."

Turning to Umiel, he spoke quietly, "Rise to the surface, contact Ariel and find out what's happening up there."

"I won't be ordered by you!" she retorted. "Well, this once only, because I'm curious." She darted off.

He climbed wearily onto the ray's back. "Fly my swift one back to the earthlings hiding place."

Josh and his father were happy that Ted could escape so they were more optimistic. "I trust Wizen. Perhaps this will be our last day here. Your mother must be frantic. If Ted has reached the surface, he can contact her." I reckon Mum and Katie will be up there, Dad. I can't see Mum waiting at home all this time." Jack started to worry, "If they did follow us, I only hope Katie isn't anywhere near the lake."

They heard Wizen ordering the ray to stop, but they waited in hiding behind some rocks until he called them. They were still well hidden, camouflaged as fish behind the seaweed. "Did Ted make it back?" they asked anxiously.

"As far as I know, yes." He cleared his throat, "I have some bad news. I don't know how to tell you this…"

"Out with it, Wizen! Nothing much worse could happen, surely," Jack said.

"Ahh, but the worst has happened. Bragh has captured your daughter."

Jack felt his worries beginning all over again. Josh spluttered, "How? When?" Wizen repeated Umiel's story.

Jack said angrily, "Why didn't they stay away?" He banged his head on the rocks until it bled.

"Dad, stop it! This won't help Katie." Josh felt sick. "Why can't we escape by the volcano?"

Wizen replied, "Because Bragh will have that guarded. Climb on the ray's back and hide under my cloak." Occasionally they would look out from under the cloak. The water was becoming darker and visibility was poor. The coldness crept into their bones.

You're late Uncle," said Mary-Anna softly.

"I have had other worries. I'll tell you when we are inside your grotto. I have two of the earthlings, the boy and his father," said Wizen.

Chapter 10

Sally recovered after a few minutes and wrapped her scarf around her bleeding arm. She managed to start the car and slowly and painfully drove back to town. She knocked on Ted's door. When he saw her, he helped her into her room. He bathed the wounds whilst she told him what had happened.

"We need to get you to hospital now. Look Sally, there are friends under the water and I am sure they will help Katie. Hang in there."

The casualty department at the hospital asked Sally if a very large cat had clawed her. She started to sob.

Ted said, "She told me she had passed out. Maybe she doesn't really remember the attack." The doctor wanted to keep her in hospital overnight, but Sally refused. She needed Ted's reassurance most of all. They returned to the motel.

After a sleepless night, Sally got out of bed and made a cup of tea. She cried for a long time, "I've lost my family."

Umiel contacted her sister, Ariel. She was shocked! "Umiel, matters are getting out of hand. Are you doing as much as you can?" Ariel enquired.

Umiel sniffed, "No more than I need. What happened to the man?"

"He's back at the motel, but the mother was injured by the sea dragon. She wouldn't stay in hospital and has gone back to the motel. I'm going to watch in her room. Just for once Umiel, think about someone else instead of yourself." She flew away. Umiel was angry, "That's all the thanks I get. As far as I'm concerned, I've done all I'm going to do. I'm not even going to pass this information on to Wizen." She was flying around aimlessly when she found herself outside Wizen's cave. "Aha! The little dog is in there. I'll wait here."

Chapter 11

Bragh dragged Katie by the hair through the water. When he arrived at his home, he shouted, "Meerlyn, is this the same girl?"

Meerlyn and Katie looked at each other. "Yes Bragh, I recognized her. She is like her brother, but he is taller." She quietly left the room.

Bragh unlocked the door at the far end of the room, "Come out, Nepta. I have a surprise for you."

Nepta was shocked to see Katie, but he remained silent. Her head hurt and she was at the point of giving up altogether, then she thought, "I must fight. If I am to see Dad and Josh again, I must persevere. I know Josh would do the same." She watched as Bragh changed back from the sea dragon. At least he didn't look so frightening.

"Have you nothing to say to each other?" Bragh laughed and slapped his son on the back. Nepta remained silent as he stared at Katie.

"Hello Nepta. We should have stayed the first time we visited." She looked at Bragh.

"Well you've got spunk. I'll say that much for you. Sit down, girl. I'll leave you and Nepta to talk." He stomped out of the room.

Nepta came up to Katie, "I can't help you this time. My father won't let me leave the house. My mother may help you." He shrugged his shoulders, "I just don't know for sure."

"Nepta, do you know where my brother and father are?"

"Yes Katie. They're with an old friend. A merman called Wizen. They are safe with him. The other man and the little dog are also with him."

"No Nepta. The man has returned to the surface." She explained his escape and the problem over Miffy.

"I didn't know there was a lava tube in that area. Umiel must have found it and kept the secret to herself," he sighed. "She's very spiteful. When she wants to help, she's marvellous, but she's usually rather selfish. I'm sorry Katie. I don't know what to do."

Bragh returned, "Go back to your room, Nepta." He locked Nepta's door. Turning to Katie, he said, "Girl, come with me."

Meerlyn appeared, "Bragh, she should have some refreshment. At least something to help the shock."

"Alright. Prepare her some food and then come and tell me when she's finished."

Meerlyn beckoned Katie to follow her through to the kitchen. A thin miserable girl was stirring something in a pot on a Glofa fire. Katie and the girl exchanged glances. Meerlyn said, "This is Gwilda. She is a very good cook and, like you, she is an earthling." Meerlyn looked into the pot and asked, "Is it ready?"

The girl replied, "Yes" and measured out a ladle of delicious smelling fish soup.

Meerlyn invited Katie to eat. "It is quite safe. You'll need to keep up your energy." Katie hesitated. She accepted the bowl and ate hungrily. She felt warmed through and much stronger. Gradually her worries eased and she felt that she didn't ever want to leave this place. She actually started to laugh.

Meerlyn was watching her. She nodded her head, "Do you feel better, Katie?"

Katie paused, "Is that my name? I don't remember anything."

Gwilda smiled, "You've been caught, Katie. You'll never leave now!" She laughed bitterly. Meerlyn took Katie's hand and called Bragh, "She's ready to go with you now." Bragh took Katie's arm and they left the house.

Chapter 12

Umiel called out to Bragh as he approached Wizen's cave. "Bragh, are you able to unlock Wizen's spell? The terrier is inside. She has been promised to me."

Bragh roared at her, "So you're the one who helped the man escape? Watch out if I catch you, Umiel!"

She laughed. "Catch me? That you'll never do!" She floated well out of his reach.

Bragh dragged Katie forward, "I know most of his spells. Let's try." He muttered some words and threw his hands at the entrance. A horrific explosion occurred. Bragh was knocked to the ground unconscious. Umiel was forced back and was deafened. She was never able to hear properly again.

Katie was thrown to the ground. When she returned to her senses, her memory had returned. She looked at Bragh. He was still unconscious. Umiel had disappeared. She stood up and observed a large clump of seaweed growing above the cave entrance. To her satisfaction, the entrance was still closed. As she floated up to the seaweed, Ariel contacted her. "Kat-ee. Walk back behind the first clump of seaweed. There you will find a mixture of coral and different coloured weeds. It is above Wizen's stove. Hide yourself there. You will keep warm. Don't move until he comes back. I must go and tell him."

Katie felt herself relaxing. She found the area. It looked like a garden. Nestling inside a gap under the coral, she immediately felt warm. Her eyes closed. Ariel skimmed over the lake, "Wizen, are you listening? Old friend, I have a story to tell."

Wizen tuned in to her thoughts. He smiled when she had finished. "Thank you Ariel. You have been a great help. We're travelling to the lava tubes tomorrow. Tell the earth people to drive around the lake until they are facing the forest. The boy and his father will come out of the forest side of the lake in the afternoon. They won't be observed from the water." Ariel was tired. She would rest now and contact Sally and Katie early tomorrow. She promptly fell asleep.

The following morning, Ted visited a doctor and explained why his skin was so marked. The doctor prescribed some cream. He sat down and faced Ted, "You are not going to believe this, but I lost a daughter many years ago in a river accident. I had a practice further north." He stopped and looked out the window. He continued after a moment, "Strange happenings and a sea dragon appeared. It killed my wife. I came here because it was quiet and it was Marie's hometown before we were married. My daughter's name was also Marie." He looked steadily at Ted, "I believe you. I've never been able to find anyone who would believe my story. I'll cancel appointments tomorrow afternoon and come with you to the police station. How would 1:00pm suit you?"

Ted agreed. He felt greatly relieved and couldn't get back to Sally quickly enough to tell her.

Sally caught up with him at the motel entrance. She started to talk, "You look happy, Ted. I'm happy too. Ariel has contacted me. We are to drive around to the forest side of the lake tomorrow afternoon."

"Sally, I can't. I have an appointment," he explained.

Sally said, "I'll go alone then. I cannot miss this opportunity."

"Look Sally, one of the police may go with you. Tell them that you've heard where they might be found."

Sally waited until the next morning, "Good luck Ted and wish me well." She had tears in her eyes. "Oh, I do hope I can see my family again."

A policewoman offered to accompany Sally and they set off.

"How much do you know, Mrs. Jenkins? And where did you hear your information?"

Sally thought hard... should she tell the policewoman what she knows? "I will answer your questions after we've found Jack and Josh."

The policewoman wasn't looking at Sally. "And if we don't find them, what then?"

"I'm sure we will."

They continued the drive in silence. Sally drove the car into the shade of the trees. The car was hidden from the lake. Sally thought the lake was shrinking. "I don't know if it's my imagination, but the lake appears smaller."

The policewoman said, "I think so too. Please don't leave the car. We'll sit here and wait."

Sally had brought sandwiches and a thermos. She had packed two blankets in the boot and had managed to have the car door replaced. After an hour had passed, she suggested they eat. They finished the sandwiches and had almost finished their coffee when the foremost trees began rustling their leaves. Ariel flew to the car, "Sally, Josh and Jack are coming. Stay in the car until you see them."

The policewoman looked stunned. "I've heard there were strange stories about this place, but I dismissed them as nonsense. No wonder you didn't want to explain."

Sally noticed two dark shapes creeping out from the shelter of the trees. "Don't make any noise, but help me bring them to the car. It's my husband and my son, Josh." The two shapes had collapsed on the ground. It was all Sally could do to keep calm. She took the blankets from the car and passed one to the policewoman. "They will be chilled and in a shocked state." When they reached Jack and Josh, Josh was shivering. Jack lay on his back, looking into the trees.

He was muttering repeatedly, "I can't believe it. I can't believe it."

"Jack, it's me, Sally. Shhh, keep quiet." She placed the blanket around Jack's shoulders. The policewoman also wrapped Josh in a blanket and carried him back to the car.

"Can you walk, Jack?" Sally asked.

He nodded his head and scrambled to his feet. "Give me your arm, Sally."

They reached the car, "I must drive away quickly. We're not safe." She accelerated and reached the road to drive back to town.

The policewoman glanced behind, "Something is happening in the water. It's foaming."

"I'm not stopping. We must drive into town. I hope we will be safe there." Sally drove even faster. They could hear a terrible roaring behind them. Jack looked back to see a sea dragon in a terrible rage. The monster had reached the edge of the lake, but something seemed to be holding it back. Its bellows faded in their ears as they sped away.

Chapter 13

Wizen and his mere people had safely escorted Jack and Josh to the lava tubes. Wizen was surprised, "Something must have happened to Bragh. He wouldn't let earthlings escape this easily." He looked at the young woman who was trembling. She was too weak to swim up the lava tube. The previous evening, he had discovered her name was Marie. She had been captured on a river fishing expedition when she was 14.

"I think I am now about 18. Bragh kept me as a housemaid for one year. I became friendly with Nepta and Bragh was angry. He changed me into a moray eel and made me leave the area. The nights were terrifying when the sea monsters prowled. I've always wondered about my parents." She cried quietly, covering her face with her hands.

"There, there my child, don't give up hope. There is an air sprite named Ariel above the water. She is helping us. I will ask her to find where your parents are living. Mary-Anna, I must return to my cave. I won't use the manta ray this time. It will take longer returning to my home. Look after Marie until I return."

Mary-Anna kissed him on the cheek, "Uncle, you are too old for all this worry. Why don't I come with you?"

"Well child, I would welcome your company, but it is very dangerous."

"No matter, I shall say my farewells. I won't be long," said Mary-Anna as she darted away.

Wizen spoke to Otriana, "Now it is time to disappear. Seek the ocean. You can disappear more easily. You are half ocean anyway."

Otriana agreed to his suggestions. She rippled smoothly, "Yes, I would like that. I have already set about shrinking my borders."

Wizen and Mary-Anna arrived back at his cave. There were no spies around, but there was a huge charred area in front of the cave. "Mmmm, I see Bragh has tried to break the spell." He laughed quietly. "Come Mary-Anna, we must slip inside quickly." He placed his hand on the door and said simply, "Opara!" The spell lifted and they entered the cave. Unnoticed, Umiel followed them inside and hid in a dark corner.

Umiel smirked, "Now to find where he has hidden the dog."

Wizen uttered, "Clota" and the spell was back in place on the entrance. "Do you wish to eat first or rest?" Wizen asked Mary-Anna.

Mary-Anna was tired. "I'll sleep here on the chair in front of the fire." She quickly dropped off to sleep. Wizen felt uneasy. Something was wrong. He searched the cave. Perhaps he should find out what Bragh was doing. It was still light outdoors. He swam up to the ceiling and uncovered a trap door. He almost fell over Katie, who shrank back in alarm. "Are you Katie, Josh's sister?" He was tired and his voice sounded gruff.

Katie whispered, "Yes."

Wizen gave up all ideas of exploring this evening. "My name is Wizen. Follow me." He opened the trap door and beckoned to Katie. She swam down into the cave. Wizen followed close behind. He muttered, "Clota!" to the trap door.

Umiel watched gleefully. So the girl hadn't been far away. Pity her hearing was so bad. She couldn't hear Wizen's magic words. She shrugged. None of it mattered. All she wanted was the dog. She deliberately kept her mind blank. She knew Wizen had sensed something and she didn't want him to discover she was hiding in his home.

"Katie, are you hungry?" asked Wizen.

"Yes, I'm starving, but I'm afraid to eat anything. Although Mr. Brown said you could be trusted."

"He told the truth. I'm delighted he returned safely. You may eat and drink in my home. The food won't harm you." He prepared a meal quickly. "Tell me what happened."

Katie enjoyed the meal. When she had finished, she explained about the explosion and then told Wizen about the events of the past few days.

"Fool! He thinks he knows everything." Wizen gave a sharp bark of laughter.

Mary-Anna awoke, "Uncle, what is wrong?" She looked at Katie, "You must be Josh's sister?"

Wizen explained, "Mary-Anna is my niece. You have another friend Katie. Just relax."

"I'm starving!" Mary-Anna went to the stove, "Have you left me any food?"

"Help yourself, my dear. Katie has just been telling me her story." Wizen repeated Katie's story to Mary-Anna whilst she ate.

Bragh was so angry and disturbed, he marched to Wizen's cave and bellowed at the entrance, "Wizen, I know you're in there. Come out! I have a score to settle with you."

Katie was disturbed, "Please don't let him in, Wizen." She burst into tears.

Mary-Anna hugged her, "He can't come in and Wizen is stronger than Bragh, but my Uncle is exhausted and needs to rest. Bragh will tire of waiting outside."

Umiel noticed agitated movement amongst the pots of seaweed. She could faintly hear some noise, "That's where Wizen would have hidden the dog, but which plant?"

Chapter 14

The young policewoman was having difficulty convincing the sergeant about what she had seen. "I've always respected you as a responsible policewoman. I cannot believe you could come up with such a story," he barked.

In a firm voice, she said, "Well, all the stories match. You've heard the Jenkins and Mr. Brown's accounts. You remarked yourself that the lake was a strange phenomenon. Come out and look for yourself."

He stood up and crossed to the window. He turned to her, "Drive me out there. I will at least see that the water is disappearing."

When they reached the lake, its size had diminished considerably. There were dead fish stranded on the dry areas.

"Remarkable!" was all the sergeant said.

When they arrived back at the station, he ordered a patrol car to watch over the area for the next few days. "At least he's suspicious, if not totally convinced." She shrugged her shoulders, "Only time will tell."

Jack and Josh had an overnight stay in hospital. The doctor who had attended Ted visited them, "I believe your story." He hesitated, "Did you see a young woman aged about 18?" He waited hopefully. They shook their heads.

The doctor said, "I believe the lake is disappearing. I gather it arises in different areas once the locals know of its dangers."

Sally was visibly shaken, "My daughter is still there." She clung to her husband. Jack could find no words of comfort.

"So is my daughter, Marie." The doctor left the room.

Ted's skin was completely healed and his strength was returning. Jack and Josh would be themselves again in a few days. Sally's arm was almost healed.

Two days later, they drove out to the lake in Ted's truck. The water had almost disappeared. Sally wanted to walk out to it, but Jack would not let her.

Josh said, "We haven't heard from Ariel. She will know what's happening."

Jack remarked, "She's possibly waiting to see where the water goes." He smiled. "Ariel will let us know where this cursed water arises next. She knows which motel we are staying at and there's nothing more to be done here."

Josh wondered if this was Wizen's idea. Then he noticed a flash of bright colours.

"Josh, it's me. Ariel. The lake is moving out to the ocean. Wizen suggested the idea to Otriana. She's like mother earth. Her domain is the water. Fetch me a map back at the motel and I'll pinpoint the area." She flew a short distance, but returned quickly. "Whatever you do, don't summon Umiel. She is not to be trusted." Ariel flew away. Josh told his father to buy a map.

Later that day, Ariel flew into Jack and Sally's room, "I have found the destination. It is a long way from here." Jack unfolded the map. Ariel took some time, "Help me. Where are we exactly?" Jack pointed to the map and pinpointed the area. Ariel traced a tiny finger north to the islands of Bermuda, "There!"

Ted asked, "Has Otriana visited there previously?"

Ariel replied, "Yes, many, many years ago." She looked again at the map, "Of course, the Bermuda Triangle."

Jack Jenkins grimaced. "It is going to be hard to find. How do we reach Katie now?"

Sally was crying. Ted realized he wouldn't see Miffy again and Josh wondered if they would ever find Katie.

Jack said, "I'll go there on my own, if necessary." He sat down and looked out the window.

"Don't give up hope," Ariel flitted around the room. "I can still contact Wizen whilst there is still some water and I have a particular friend, the West Wind. He will help us anytime." Their spirits lifted.

"We might as well go home then?" Ted queried.

Ariel shook her head, "Not yet. The water will take a further two to three days to disappear. I'll keep in touch. When the water has entirely disappeared, then you can return to your homes. My West Wind friend will help you. I'll leave you now and tell you more tomorrow."

She was gone so quickly. Nobody really saw her leave.

Chapter 15

After Bragh left Wizen's cave, Wizen packed Mary-Anna and Katie off to bed. He could still feel something wrong in the cave. He glanced across at the pot plants. He should check on the little terrier. He came across to the bench and moved the plants. A thought came to him... was someone watching? Grinning, he pulled the tiniest plant to the front and smoothed its leaves. If anyone else touched it, they would burn their fingers. He flopped into a chair and pretended to be asleep.

Umiel was cautious. Wizen had probably set a trap. The plant he had been stroking was too obvious. She watched Wizen until she thought he was in a deep sleep. Creeping over to the pot plants, she was so busy watching Wizen, she didn't notice the creeper plant stalking her. She stood still. That was her last mistake!

The plant sent out a tendril, coiling around her body and squeezed her tightly. She screamed until her breath gave out. Her tiny body slumped down. The tendril whipped back to the main plant and swallowed her!

Wizen sprang out of his chair. Whatever had been disturbing his thoughts had gone. He went over to the plants. His carnivorous weed looked plump. It had found a tasty meal. He had an unpleasant thought. Could it have been Umiel? He sighed. Poor Umiel. He returned to his chair. This time he fell into a deep sleep.

When he awoke the following morning, Katie and Mary-Anna were preparing breakfast.

Mary-Anna was singing, "Good morning Uncle. Are you rested?"

He stroked his beard, "Yes I am, thank you. Mmmm... that smells good."

They chatted and laughed during breakfast while Mary-Anna was clearing away the dishes. He beckoned Katie over to the pot plants, "I have a little friend here. You may like to see her." Katie was intrigued. She couldn't imagine what was so special about different types of seaweed. She watched while Wizen picked up a pot and patted the leaves. Slowly the plant changed shape.

"Miffy!" She laughed with delight. "Oh Miffy, you poor little dog. What an experience you have had." She cuddled the little terrier. Miffy started to bark.

"Ahh!" Wizen placed his hand on Miffy's snout. Immediately the barking stopped, "We can't allow that. It's too dangerous." He looked at Katie, "While she is in here, I'll leave her in her natural form. Outside she will have to be transformed."

Katie played with Miffy for a short time. "Mr. Brown loves her so much. He must have given up hope of ever seeing her again."

"Well, we will try to return Miffy, along with you and one other."

Mary-Anna queried, "When do you plan to start Uncle?"

Wizen wondered if he should check on Otriana's withdrawal first. He said, "Otriana must nearly be in her new situation. I must tune into Ariel as soon as possible. I will leave you for a while. Don't leave the cave." He ascended to the trap door and muttered, "Opara!" and disappeared.

He waited and listened by the door. When he was sure it was safe, he swam some distance away. Hiding behind some rocks, he waited again. He was alone. He whistled for the manta ray, but she didn't appear. Looking ahead, he discovered a rock wall. He followed its boundary. The rock wall enclosed the cave. "One up to you, Bragh!" He was annoyed. "Now to try and break through."

Chapter 16

The water took two days to disappear. Ariel was disturbed. She told the earthlings, "There must be a spell. I can't reach Wizen.

The Jenkins family were very anxious. Ariel suggested they return to their homes and she would ask the West Wind to watch over them. Ted hoped he would see Miffy soon.

They set off on the long drive home. Ted had a quick visit with the doctor. They exchanged addresses and phone numbers. Ted then visited the police station and informed the sergeant they were returning home.

The sergeant cleared his throat, "I'm sorry I mistrusted you, but I now believe that something occurred for which there is no reasonable explanation. Good bye and good luck!"

Wizen tried every spell breaker he could think of. Nothing worked. Then he swam up to the full height of the wall. A net covered the area. Perhaps he could burrow under? He had a brain wave... this was a task for Miffy. He returned to the cave and explained what had happened.

Mary-Anna and Katie both demanded to come too, "Now Uncle, this is the perfect opportunity for you to come back and live with us."

"This time, my dear, I agree with you."

Miffy tunnelled away at the foot of the wall and soon a hole appeared. The three of them took turns in scraping away the sand. Eventually the hole was big enough to crawl through.

Wizen whistled and the manta ray appeared. "It seems Bragh couldn't close off all avenues of escape." Wizen rolled a large rock over the hole. "Just in case! Now let's go quickly." Wizen handed Katie his cloak.

They all climbed on the ray's back. Katie hid Miffy in Wizen's cloak and cuddled her tightly. They sped swiftly to the mountains. Wizen kept looking behind him. No one appeared to be following them. Mary-Anna suggested that Bragh might have gone ahead.

"I think not. He imagines we're trapped in the cave," Wizen said.

As they approached the mountains, the mer people came out to meet them. They didn't look happy. "Bragh has destroyed all the lava tubes and some of our people are badly injured. He's gone on a wild rampage and stirred up the sea monsters. Nowhere is safe. You had better keep moving."

Wizen called a halt just long enough to collect Marie. He directed the ray to keep close to the base of the mountains. They flew for about an hour. Wizen stopped the ray and they all dismounted. He stroked the ray's head and sent her away.

"We'll have to climb. We're near the smallest peak. Just down the other side, we should sight some whales.

They will help you back to land. I want to travel as far as we can before nightfall." They formed a single line and followed Wizen up the mountain. It was bitterly cold and, in spite of the exercise, they were shivering.

When they had climbed about a third of the distance, he suggested they stop as Katie and Marie's legs were aching. Mary-Anna had some merman bread and dried fruit. She shared this with the others. There was just enough for one more meal. Wizen nodded, "We must move on. I want to find some shelter before it gets dark."

They kept climbing until they had reached a point half way up the mountain. Some rocks had fallen and formed a three-sided shelter. "We'll stay here tonight. I can place a spell over the entrance. We should keep warm and it will be reasonably safe."

During the night, sea monsters prowled around the rocks. Katie could see them. They had green scales, black talons and huge fangs.

By morning, Wizen undid the spell. He listened. After a few moments, he looked out, and sensed eyes watching. Turning to the others, he said quietly, "Katie and Marie, I have to transform you. I think Bragh is nearby. Certainly there are spies."

He picked up Miffy and stroked her. He changed her into a tiny starfish. He waved his hands over Katie and Marie. They became so small, he could hold them in his hands. He whispered, "Hide yourselves. Katie, hold Miffy." He looked at Mary-Anna, "My dear, you don't really need to continue. You should return home."

Mary-Anna was stubborn, "Certainly not! I want to see this through. I'll create a diversion and meet you on the other side." She glided out from the shelter. She appeared to be accompanied by two girls. Wizen waited in the rock shelter. A shadow passed. It was Bragh! He heard the roar as Bragh chased after Mary-Anna. She would surely give him a chase.

Ariel tuned in to Wizen. She caught up with Ted on the outskirts of Briesdale. He stopped the truck. "Wizen has Katie and Miffy. They are returning to collect Marie and their escape will be arranged shortly. Keep in touch with the West Wind. I'll send messages."

Ted almost cried with relief. He turned the truck towards the town. His first visit was to the doctor's surgery.

Chapter 17

Wizen looked around him. The mountain summit was barely visible. "Otriana, you have reached your new destination. Well done, my lady!"

He kept close to the mountain face as he drifted upwards. Schools of fish swam past. He wondered how successful Mary-Anna had been at luring Bragh away. He restored Katie, Marie and Miffy to normal. "It's dangerous, but I still have a few tricks." He swam around the trio chanting. He explained, "You're in a magic circle. Only I can undo the spell. Follow me."

They came across a school of fish and joined in the crowd. Gradually, the water felt warmer. There was less seaweed and the water appeared to be getting shallower. Wizen indicated he would swim ahead and he left the group. His tail swept the sandy floor. Cautiously, he broke the surface. An island ahead of him showed a village and mountains in the background. There were earthlings at the water's edge.

"Good!" he muttered. He waited until the trio appeared and broke the spell. Marie dragged herself onto the beach and lay still. She couldn't understand the language. The villagers were amazed. This black-haired girl appeared exhausted. She slowly stood up. Her grey eyes pleading. Wizen turned to Katie, "Now you follow and…"

There was no sign of Katie and Miffy. Bragh had been behind Wizen watching and waiting for his chance. He was seething with anger. The mer girl had fooled him. He smiled grimly. He had dealt with her. When he had caught her, he had thrown her to the sea monsters. If he could outwit this old merman, he would have revenge. He knew Wizen wasn't aware of him following. Pity that he had lost one earthling, but he had this child and a dog.

I suppose I should take the dog back to Coralie. She's probably forgotten about it by now, Bragh thought to himself. He held Katie and Miffy firmly in his grasp and descended to the depths. Katie had fainted. Miffy barked. Her sharp terrier instincts had alerted her to danger.

Wizen was so tired. He lay in the shallow water and thought to himself... after all that travelling, I have failed. He closed his eyes. The West Wind skittered over the water, "Wizen, wake up! I have a message from Ariel." Wizen slept on. The Wind blew itself out to sea. It would try again later.

Bragh had arrived at the mountains. He sought the rock shelter. He pushed Katie inside and sealed the entrance. Carrying Miffy, he swam on. He was a powerful swimmer, but his muscles were starting to ache and he was tiring. He must rest. He gently dropped to the ocean floor and tied Miffy with a seaweed cord to a rock. He would sleep now. He dropped on to a soft, sandy patch and instantly fell asleep.

Miffy took a long time, but she eventually chewed through the cord. In a frenzy, she attacked Bragh... first his legs, then his arms. He awoke roaring and tried to catch her, but she was too fast. She kept darting and biting, blood flowing through the water, but he couldn't catch her. She sensed other predators in the area. She turned and swam quickly away.

Hiding behind some rocks, she watched a group of sea snakes attacking Bragh. He was forced down to the seabed and never moved. The snakes departed, hissing amongst themselves.

Miffy waited and watched. The little terrier edged over to his body and sniffed. Bragh's eyes were open, but they were glazing over. She was too slow. His left hand held her and crushed her little body. She whimpered and laid still.

Chapter 18

Katie came to her senses. Wherever she was, it was dark. She looked for Miffy. Apparently, she was alone. She was almost insane with terror. The long night had passed. The first grey light of dawn appeared through the cracks and Katie realized she was in the rock shelter. She could hear someone moving about outside. Katie started screaming.

"Hush Katie, hush. It's Wizen."

She calmed down, "Bragh has put a spell on the entrance. Oh Wizen, let me out please!"

"I'm trying, Katie. I just have to find the right words."

The morning passed before Wizen found the right spell and Katie tumbled into his arms. "Come, we'll go back to the mere people. We both need rest." He took her hand, "I feel something has happened. Not good, but a sense of evil has gone." He shook his head.

They swam at a leisurely pace, keeping close together. When they reached the area where Bragh lay, Wizen nodded, "Your time was up! You've created too much evil and…"

Katie screamed, "Its Miffy! He killed her!" Katie cradled Miffy's little broken body.

Wizen turned Katie to face Bragh, "The little terrier put up a fight. Look at the bites. What she started, the sea snakes finished." He smiled grimly. "Perhaps revenge from some or all of his changelings." He waved his hand and muttered some words. Bragh sank into the seabed. Blood-red seaweed eventually grew over the area. "It will mark his burial place, should Meerlyn wish to visit."

"What would you like me to do with Miffy?" He gently removed the little dog from Katie's arms.

"Not here," she sobbed, "Not with that thing. Don't bury her here, please Wizen."

"Very well. She can lay at rest with my people." They swam on, both hungry and tired. The mere people came out to meet them.

"Have you found Mary-Anna?" queried Wizen.

Mary-Anna's mother, Margarite, was Wizen's sister and Mary-Anna looked just like her. Margarite's eyes were red from weeping. "We are burying her amongst the coral," she sighed. "What's left of her, that is? The sea dragons tore her apart."

Wizen signed, "My poor Mary-Anna". He was silent for some time. Then he put his arm around Margarite and asked gently if Miffy could rest with her.

Margarite replied, "Ah yes, that would be fine." Wizen placed Miffy with Mary-Anna and they covered the bodies with fine, silver sand.

Chapter 19

Wizen and Katie stayed with the mere people overnight. Wizen had some final arrangements to make. He contacted Ariel and asked her to arrange for Katie's parents to hire a boat. He gave her the compass directions they would need so they could meet Katie. Wizen whistled for the manta ray and they sped straight to the volcano.

Wizen said to Katie, "You have travelled this way before. Do you feel brave enough to try it again?"

"Anything to go home, Wizen." She was scared, but at least it was a way of escape.

He handed her a packet of biscuits, "They are called Fofar. They will dry out when you reach land."

She took them from him, "What are these for?"

Wizen smiled, "They will help you to forget these terrible days. Give one to everybody. I'm going to Meerlyn now to tell her the news about Bragh. I will ease Nepta's mind that you are all safe." He hugged Katie and kissed her on the forehead. "Off you go. The volcano is rumbling." He watched sadly, as she was borne upwards.

Katie's parents were nervous. They didn't know what to expect.

Josh said, "Don't worry. Wizen would have protected Katie."

They had been waiting about thirty minutes when ripples began to appear on the surface. A sound of rushing water was heard. They watched the ripples with nervous anticipation.

A huge spurt of water broke the surface and Katie was thrown upwards. Her father dived in and caught Katie. He supported her back to the boat. Josh and Sally pulled Katie into the boat. Jack clambered in immediately after. Sally wrapped a blanket around Katie and hugged her daughter closely. Jack started the outboard motor and they returned to the jetty where Ted was waiting. When they were all seated in Ted's truck, she miserably recounted her experiences underwater and cried from time to time. When she tried to tell Ted about Miffy, she broke down completely.

"I think I understand, Katie." Ted spoke quietly. "Ariel told me part of the story. My brave little Miffy." His voice broke.

Katie explained about the Fofar biscuits. They practically all spoke at once.

"Oh yes, let's forget all about it."

They all munched on a biscuit. Forever after, the Jenkins family had a fear of the sea, which they could never explain to their friends, so they chose to move to the mountains.

Ted was lonely. He decided to buy a little terrier. Jilly always reminded him of Miffy, the dog he had once loved very dearly.

Ariel had been busy. Marie and her father had been reunited. He gave up his medical practice and devoted his time to healing his daughter. It took Marie a long time to put the horrors of her underwater life behind her.

Wizen visited Bragh's house. Only Nepta was home.

"My mother and Coralie are out seeking news of my father." He stopped speaking and looked intently at Wizen, "Is my father dead?"

Wizen nodded. Nepta was silent for some time, and then he squared his shoulders, "I guess I'm the man of the house now!"

Meerlyn entered the front door. Coralie was close behind her. "You have brought me news about Bragh, Wizen?" She sat down. "I know..." she hesitated. "He's dead, isn't he? He was a very difficult man. My life will be easier now..." She drew Nepta towards her, ". . . and easier for my son." She had a sudden thought and asked Wizen, "Did the earthlings get away safely?"

"Yes they did. I've given them Fofar biscuits. They won't remember their visit to Otriana."

He sensed something stirring in Coralie. He turned towards her. Her black eyes were gleaming. She was smiling, but her mouth had a cruel twist, "Oh yes they will!" she muttered.

THE END

www.ingramcontent.com/pod-product-compliance
Lightning Source LLC
LaVergne TN
LVHW020434080526
838202LV00055B/5187